LEGO NINJAGO
Masters of Spinjitzu

MASTERS OF SPINJITZU

ADAPTED BY TRACEY WEST

SCHOLASTIC INC.
NEW YORK   TORONTO   LONDON   AUCKLAND
SYDNEY   MEXICO CITY   NEW DELHI   HONG KONG

ISBN 978-0-545-40114-2

LEGO, the LEGO logo, the Brick and Knob configurations and the Minifigure are trademarks of the LEGO Group. ©2012 The LEGO Group. Produced by Scholastic Inc. under license from the LEGO Group. Published by Scholastic Inc. SCHOLASTIC and associated logos are trademarks and/or registered trademarks of Scholastic Inc.

30 29 28 27 26 25 24 23   16 17/0

Printed in the U.S.A.   40
First printing, January 2012

MEET THE TEAM

As the sun rose over Ninjago, four young ninja pulled a wagon up a tall mountain. They were on a quest to find the Scythe of Quakes, one of the Four Weapons of Spinjitzu.

In the wagon sat Sensei Wu, their teacher.

Kai, the ninja in red, was the newest member of the team.

"So, where did Sensei find you three?" Kai asked the others.

"I was testing my limits," answered Cole, the ninja in black. "I climbed the tallest mountain without any tools. But when I reached the top, Sensei Wu was there, drinking his tea."

"I was testing my invention," said Jay, the ninja in blue.

Jay had made a pair of wings. He tried to fly . . . only to crash and find Sensei Wu there. He was waiting on a nearby rooftop, drinking his tea.

"And I was testing myself," said Zane, the quiet ninja in white.

Zane was meditating at the bottom of a frozen lake. And somehow . . . Sensei Wu was there underwater, drinking his tea!

THE PLAN

"Stop!" Sensei Wu cried suddenly.

The ninja came to a halt. A large canyon stretched out in front of them. Skeleton warriors were digging into the side of the mountain.

"The Caves of Despair," Sensei said. "Samukai must be close to unearthing the Scythe of Quakes."

"Remember, do not use the Weapon," Sensei Wu warned. "For its power —"

"Yeah, yeah, yeah!" Jay said. He had heard this from Sensei before. "Its power is too much for us mortals." He turned to his friends. "All right guys, let's chop-socky this lemonade stand! Cole, you got the plan?"

"Sure do," Cole replied. "First, we — hey, where's Kai?"

Kai hadn't waited to hear the plan. The ninja saw him sneaking past the skeleton warriors in the canyon.

"Let's go!" Jay cried.

STEALTH ATTACK

Jay, Cole, and Zane jumped into the canyon. They saw rocks coming out of the caves on a conveyor belt. The skeleton warriors checked each rock, looking for the Scythe of Quakes.

One of the warriors spotted Kai! But before he could cry out, the other ninja jumped him.

Bam! Pow! Crunch! Cole, Jay, and Zane made sure the warrior couldn't sound the alarm.

Kai hid behind some big rocks. He looked up at a tall tower in the middle of the canyon. Inside he saw Samukai, King of the Underworld!

"The map!" Kai cried. The map showed where the Four Weapons of Spinjitzu were hidden. Samukai had stolen it from Kai's blacksmith shop.

Nearby, two skeleton commanders were checking rocks on the conveyor belt. Cole, Jay, and Zane slid right under them!

But Kruncha and Nuckal didn't notice.

"I found something!" Nuckal cried, holding up a rock.

"That's another rock, you bonehead!"
Kruncha yelled.

"But it's shaped like a donut," Nuckal said.
"I wonder if it tastes like one?"

Crunch! Nuckal bit down hard into the
rock. *"Ow!"*

Kai climbed to the top of the tall tower. Cole, Jay, and Zane joined him.

Jay smacked Kai on the head. "What's the matter with you?"

"*Shhh!*" Kai warned. He nodded toward a hole in the tower roof. Inside the tower, Samukai was reading the map.

"It's upside down!" Jay realized. "They're digging in the wrong spot!"

THE SCYTHE OF QUAKES

"The Golden Weapon is near," Zane realized. He tied a shuriken to a rope and tossed it down the hole. Samukai didn't see it. The shuriken grabbed the map, and Zane pulled it up through the hole.

"There's no time to waste," Kai said. He did a backflip off the tower and ran off.

"What is it with that guy?" Jay asked. "Always in a rush!"

The ninja raced after Kai toward the spot where the Scythe of Quakes was hidden. A big rock blocked the entrance. Cole, Jay, Kai, and Zane worked together to push it aside.

The Scythe of Quakes lit up the dark cave. The Weapon lay on top of a statue of a dragon's head.

"That is so cool!" Jay cried. His voice echoed through the cave.

"*Shh!* Not so loud!" Cole warned. He jumped on top of the statue, grabbed the Weapon, and tossed it to Kai. "Now let's sneak out while those boneheads are still busy," he said.

Behind them, the statue's mouth slowly began to open. . . .

AN ESCAPE GONE WRONG

The ninja walked outside of the cave . . . right into Samukai and his warriors!

Samukai opened all four of his arms wide. Each bony hand held a sharp dagger. The ninja drew their swords and charged ahead with a battle cry.

"Hii yaa!"

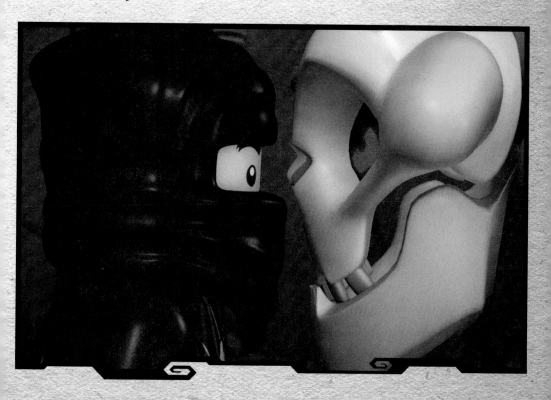

Cole, Jay, Kai, and Zane fought their way through the army of skeleton warriors.

"There's too many of them!" Kai yelled, whacking a skeleton with his sword.

"Let me handle it!" Jay called out. He jumped into the middle of a gang of warriors.

Suddenly, Jay stopped. He looked at the warriors in front of him. Some held long staffs. Others were spinning weapons above their heads.

"Guys, it's just like Sensei's training course!" he realized.

All four ninja had practiced on the course. They wanted to learn Spinjitzu. But so far, none of them could spin like Sensei Wu.

"Over the planks!" Jay cried, jumping from warrior to warrior, knocking them down.

"Dodge the swords!" Jay somersaulted over the heads of the sword-waving warriors.

"Here comes the dummy!" he finished, spinning into another warrior.

MASTERS OF SPINJITZU

Jay kept spinning faster . . . and faster . . . and faster . . . until he became a glowing blue tornado.

"Spinjitzu!" Cole cried.

"Jay, what's the key?" Kai called out.

"I'm just going through the motions!" Jay yelled back.

Kai remembered the training. He jumped. He somersaulted. He spun . . . and he became a spinning tornado!

Cole and Zane got it, too. Soon all four ninja were using Spinjitzu, taking out skeletons left and right.

ENTER THE DRAGON

"Retreat!" Samukai shouted.

The four ninja chased Samukai and his army out of the cave.

Cole flexed his muscles. "Guess they didn't want any more of these babies," he bragged.

Then they all heard a strange, growling noise behind them.

"Um, didn't Sensei say there was a guardian protecting the Weapon?" Zane asked.

The dragon statue wasn't a statue at all — it was a real dragon! The huge beast slowly rose to its feet.

"Is th-th-that what I think it is?" Cole asked nervously.

"I sense we will not be able to spin our way out of this," Zane remarked.

The dragon reared back, opened its mouth, and blasted the ninja with a blazing orange flame.

"Aaaaaaaaaaaah!" The ninja screamed as the blast knocked them down.

Cole, Jay, Kai, and Zane raced away as hot dragon fire licked at their heels.

Kai got a gleam in his eye. He removed the cloth that covered the Scythe of Quakes.

"Bad idea, Kai!" Jay warned. "Sensei told us not to use it."

But Kai didn't listen. He ran up to the dragon.

Bam! Kai swung the Scythe and brought it down on the cave floor. The ground began to tremble and crack. The dragon lost its balance and fell.

"We've got to escape!" Cole yelled.

TEAMWORK

The four ninja raced away. But the dragon wasn't down for long. It started to chase them.

"We can use Spinjitzu!" Cole cried. He started to spin, and his friends did the same.

Soon four glowing tornadoes were swirling up the cave walls, heading for an opening in the ceiling.

Cole, Jay, Kai, and Zane escaped through the hole before the dragon could catch them.

"That was so awesome!" Cole cheered. He gave Kai a high-five.

"Yes! We are unbelievable!" Kai yelled.

"We are the best," Zane said proudly.

"Did you see that?" Jay asked. "I was like, *pow! Bam!*"

Sensei Wu joined the four ninja. "Kai, you are part of a team now. Do not forget that." Sensei turned around. "Come! There are three Weapons left."

The four ninja followed Sensei Wu out of the canyon. Now that they had mastered Spinjitzu, they were ready for their next adventure.